WILLY AND THE CLOUD

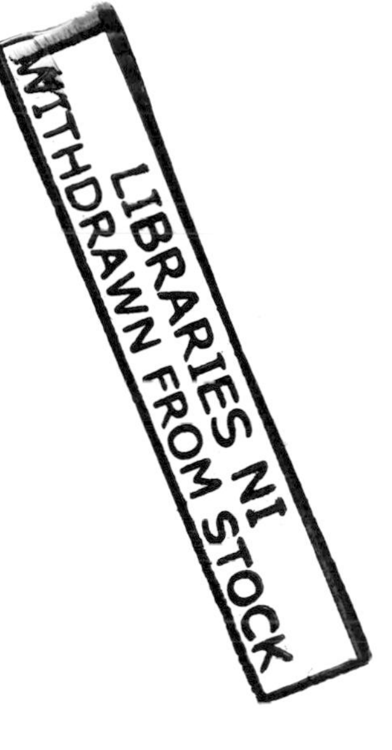

ANTHONY BROWNE

It all began on a warm, sunny day when Willy
decided to go to the park.
There wasn't a cloud in the sky when he set off.
(Well, just a little, tiny one.)

That's a bit annoying, he thought.

The cloud seemed to be following him.

What's going on?

I think it's gone…

Yes, it has gone. Phew!

(But Willy was wrong…)

At the park everyone seemed to be having great fun.

Willy just shivered.

So he went home.

Why was the cloud following him? What could he do?

"Hello," said Willy. "Is that the police?"
"Yes, sir. How can I help?"
"W-well, you see, I'm – I'm being followed."
"I see, sir. Who by? Can you give me a description?"
"Er … well, that's a bit difficult. It's – it's a cloud."
"You're being followed by a CLOUD, sir?"
"Yes – a BIG cloud…"
Willy heard the horrible sound of laughing policemen.
"Oh, dear," he said and put down the phone.

This cloud is awful, thought Willy. *How can I get rid of it?* The room was getting darker and darker, so he turned on the light and closed the curtains.

After a couple of hours Willy nervously peeped out of the window. "Fantastic – it's gone!" he shouted.

(But he was wrong...)

Willy felt miserable. The house was becoming very hot. He could hardly breathe. There seemed to be no air. He heard loud, rumbling noises outside and slowly he began to feel angry. Eventually he could stand it no longer. He rushed outside...

I'VE HAD ENOUGH! YOU'RE NOTHING BUT A CLOUD MADE OF TINY LITTLE DROPLETS OF WATER AND AIR! GO AWAY!

Everything went quiet. What was happening?
Was the cloud crying? It felt rather wonderful.
The soft, cool rain was delicious.
Willy felt like singing … and even dancing!

After a while the rain stopped and the sun came out.
I think I'll try the park again, thought Willy.

And this time, when he got there

EVERYONE was happy!